Molly Malice
in
Alterland

We Wake Up Screaming

David E. Manuel

Persimmon Alley Press
Arlington, VA
www.persimmonalleypress.com

Published by Persimmon Alley Press
Cover design by David E. Manuel

All images and cover photographs
property of OWNER
or from Publick Domaine

ISBN: 978-0-9991366-8-3

Contents

Introduction

I think it's safe to say that a lot of us in the United States have been driven over the edge by the last few years. It's not a partisan divide, either; people of all political persuasion are increasingly acting like lunatics. And who can blame them? The best explanation I've seen of what's transpired is that we really are living in a simulation, and the programmers got bored and decided to tweak the program with some random insanity.

I mean, how else to make sense of things when the president's son-in-law says the key to understanding the first family is to read *Alice in Wonderland*? Of course, I suspect he's basing that on having seen the movie, not reading the book. That's even scarier—just who is Johnny Depp playing, then?

Even odder, I've been adapting John Tenniel's original drawings for *Alice in Wonderland* and *Through the Looking Glass* into disturbing caricatures of the current madness for some time, well before reading that I'm not the only one thinking we've fallen down the rabbit hole.

Those Tenniel drawings are all in the public domain, by the way, so they're fair game for repurposing. That's good news to those of us who lack artistic talent and who don't have a publisher willing to set us up with a high-priced illustrator because our name's Dan Brown or John Lithgow. Actually, "don't have a publisher" suffices, it turns out.

These days, anybody with a computer, software like GIMP and an Amazon account can piece together insulting satires and make them available to be ignored on the Internet. It's a brave new world, and, wow, what people it has in it.

So flip through this thin volume. You'll find some illustrations that may amuse you and a few words of accompaniment. If any of it rings familiar; well, you've probably lived through the same weird shit as the rest of us and, like us, are hoping deep inside it's an elaborate practical joke.

Gotta run now. The nurse just announced it's time for meds and lights out.

See you on the other side.

Maybe.

The Author

October 2020

Molly Malice in Alterland

1. The Bunny Trail

'Twas a sunny day in the Republic of Lubberlay,
spring in the air and summer on its way.
Townsfolk gathered in annual celebration by the
founder's statue, lifting spirits and libations.
Leading light and lady Felicity Dillary exposited
on virtue, a moving oration welcomed and
applauded by everyone.

Well, almost everyone.

"What a know-it-all," thought little Molly Malice.
"And pushy, too! I do not like her."
But what could she do? "I will have
to think on it," she mused. Into
a nearby meadow she wandered
and pondered a bit to no avail.
The field was pleasant, flowers
abundant, and a bunny hopped by.
Or was it a hare? She had never
been able to tell them apart.
"But I do declare,"
the rabbit announced
while fingering his fob.
"I've much to do," and
off he did dart.

"Oh, this is odd," Molly cried. "Such a finely dressed rabbit in this rustic countryside. What business might he have, with clothes so smart?"

She hastened to pursue. Through the field she chased, then into a wood. The trees grew thick. She stumbled on a root, then stood and let out a sob.

Her haircombe, gone! Passed down from Oma! Finest ivory and all!

"Ooh, Felicity Dillary, what you made me do! Now I've lost my heirloom on account of you!"

Molly looked all around but to no avail, then noticed a hole in the ground, exhaled.

"I'll bet it's down there!" She knelt and peered. The hole was broad and deep. She reached and reached.

2

Her finger brushed something. A bristle, a tine!
She reached further and grasped it, then down she
slid.

Down and down and down some more, she slid far
below the woodland floor. "How strange," she
thought. "I've never fallen down a rabbit hole
before!"

Then through the hole and farther she fell,
tumbling in air until she landed with a "Thump!"

"Drumpf!" she grunted, then picked herself up,
brushed herself off, pulled back her hair, inserted
her comb and looked about. All around was a
landscape like none she'd ever seen. "What place
can this be?"

"Alterland, dearie," came a voice from behind. She
whirled but saw only an empty tree.

"Who's there? Show yourself! I'll count to three!"
She crossed her arms and made a pout.

"Patience, my girl. I'm right before your eyes. It's just, I'm hard to see."

And slowly she made out a creature quite odd with the body of a cat and a head all bloated and fat.

"And just what did you say this place is?" Molly shot him a glance.

"Well, little girl," the creature drawled, "'tis Alterland you're in, by chance."

"And where would that be, exactly?"

"It's a place of alternatives, to state it quite factually." The cat rubbed its fat head against a branch. "Or, alternative facts, actually."

"Alternative facts? What might those be?"

"You'll discover soon enough. Just follow the path through field and rough."

The cat vanished with a wink, or was it a blink?

"How rude to leave with a riddle," Molly muttered. But then she made out the faintest track braced by reeds that fluttered in a soft breeze. "I'll make my way then."

"If you please," came the cat's voice disembodied in the trees.

Molly set out with a determined gait down a path sometimes crooked sometimes straight. The sun shone bright, which seemed a bit odd in a land at the bottom of a rabbit's abode. Yet onward Molly strode, through hill and dale and into a vale of broad leaves and mushrooms as large as whales!

"Toadstools!"

She stopped in her tracks. The word had wafted from above like a cloud, and, indeed, a cloud of smoke descended as a shroud. She stretched on her tiptoes to see what rested atop this gargantuan . . .

"Toadstool, you see. Voila!" A caterpillar sat there perched with a hookah.

"But you are no toad," Molly exclaimed.

"And you are no welcome guest, but do I complain?"

"Well, yes, you just did."

The caterpillar sighed, exhaling a pungent ring of smoke. "Might I inquire then, little artichoke, what cause you have to disturb me so? Uninvited, I'll add."

"I am delighted to tell. It was you who spoke first. And second, as well."

"Merely to correct a misperception." It gave it's head a sad shake.

"I said nothing in error."

"But it's a common mistake, taking toadstool for mushroom. I simply averted a *faux pas* you were certain to make!"

"Then if you are so smart, can you answer me this? Do alternative facts exist? Do you know?"

The caterpillar frowned, something not to be missed. "Why, who told you so?"

"Don't laugh," Molly answered. "A cat in a tree."

"Oh, that fat-headed feline can be quite misleading." The creature inhaled, then exhaled a dark puff. "He's the bane of Darjeeling, makes up all sorts of stuff. All Alterland knows he's not to be trusted."

"Then this is Alterland?"

The bug looked disgusted. "What else would it be? And who are you to ask?"

"Molly Malice," she answered defiantly.

It lowered its head in a manner of condescension. "Then take your own direction and ask her the question."

"What? Ask who?"

"Why, this Molly Malice you refer to."

"That's me!" Molly shouted.

The caterpillar winced. "Oh, you misunderstood then. But perhaps I misspoke. So confusing misusing a 'who' for a 'whom.'"

"What a silly centipede you are." But her ankles and toes were beginning to ache from the strain. Again she exclaimed, "I must know of these ulterior facts."

"Why didn't you say so?" Its sunglasses glinted. "I'll give you a riddle in which they are hidden.

Be ever so good whenever you're able.
Don't make up stories or listen to fables.
Endeavor forever to be upright and stable.
Avoid sweets and eat all your vege-tables."

"That's not how you pronounce 'vegetables,'" Molly retorted. "And it sounds quite silly, like what I'd expect from Felicity Dillary."

"Eureka!" erupted from the caterpillar. "And there you have it. 'Tis exactly the opposite of advice we all merit!"

"I see!" Molly brightened. "Ulterior facts!"

"Alternative, dearie." The caterpillar seemed weary. "And now if you'll be on your way, you'll find them in abundance today."

As if answering a command the edges of the toadstool curled up grimly into a sort of puffy tulip shape, smoke emanating out the top as from a chimney. Molly lost her grip and fell back amid the vegetation, expelling another "drumpf!" in punctuation!

"How annoyingly rude!" she declared, then stood, felt through her hair. "But at least my comb is still there!"

2. Beasts, To Say the Least

A strange sound permeated the air.

Grrrr. Grrrr. Gruff, gruff, grrka.
  Snuff, snuffle, gruff, mazurka.

Molly bent low and crept toward the commotion. From behind a large bush she peered. A giant, four-legged beast rubbed its snout in the grass before her, muttering.

Grrruff me gon hrrrt ya mm vishuss nnd mnnnly!

She picked up a stick and stepped out to face it. "You startled me, beast. Stop this racket at once!"

Its eyes locked on the stick. She waved it; the eyes traced it, hypnotically. Molly feared the beast's size, but dared indulge her curiosity. "And what manner of creature are you?"

"Pwrrrrfll wlllfff mm mmeee!"

"Wolf, indeed! Well, what name are you called?"

"*Arrrrtokrrrrcy.*"

"Your diction is horrid," Molly noted, appalled.

The beast snarled. "*Yrrr gtt tew mmmch lllbrty!*"

It grimaced. "*Mmm ssee yew mmmwled!*"

But she laughed. "Why you're merely a puppy!" She hurled the stick out into the field. The creature's head followed, and then the rest, stumbling as it reeled. "Such a fat puppy, too. I don't think I'll have trouble getting away from you!"

She turned to be on her way, butted into a giant rock and fell with dismay. "What a bump. Now my head is sore and I'll have a bruise. But this boulder was not here before!"

"Oh, you are obtuse!" It seemed someone had spoken, although "whined" would be more precise. Yet not a soul could she see; perhaps behind the precipice? She crawled to its side, peered around, but nothing except more empty ground. "Show yourself, no need to hide."

"I am here before you, little scamp."

"A stone that talks? What next, a magic lamp?"

"Oh, woe to me to endure such sarcasm from a tramp!"

Then Molly looked up and saw, 'twas no boulder, it had a head on its shoulder.

"Why, you're a turtle standing erect!"

It glowered down at her. "What did you expect?"

She pondered a moment, then said with a spin, "Certainly not a terrapin."

"First you hurl a stick to torment my pet, then hurl insults at me, little strumpet."

"So you call me 'tramp,' then 'strumpet' in a twist. I thought you reptile, not misogynist."

"And yet she persists." It glowered. "I'll have you know, I wield critical power. 'Tis me is all that stands between civilization and anarchy."

"With your pet dog, Autocracy?"

"Why, that is but a synonym for 'democracy'!"

Its head receded a bit in its shell. "But it is beneath my dignity to dispute political science with one so persnickety."

Molly's cheeks reddened in rage. "Are you always so disagreeable, or is it just women you outrage with insults so feeble."

"Little else is warranted, I'll wager," it said with a haughtily-raised eyebrow. "Young ladies like you are all socialists by nature."

"And yet I know better than you the difference between democracy and autocracy, socialism and anarchy."

"A student of letters, it's true, might so argue." It stretched its neck to a peculiar angle. "Yet I'll reckon you're new here. True?"

"If by 'here' you mean Alterland, well, yes, I've just arrived."

"By accident, I'll surmise."

"I was following a rabbit and fell into its warren."

"Ah, yes, I know the beast of which you speak. A creature once noble, sadly now of all morals barren."

"Then a cat alluded to this land of alternatives . . ."

"Unreliable associates, felines."

". . . and a caterpillar promised freedom from silly pejoratives."

"Oho, so the worm has turned," added the tortoise dryly. "But you have here much to learn, little dearie. Thus follow me to one who might explain more clearly."

Slowly it turned its great carcass around and began to creep forward with a groaning sound.

"But your doggie," Molly called. "Will you leave unleashed your horrid little gargoyle?"

"He has yet more greenage to snuffle and soil."

Slowly the armored beast trudged forward, muttering as it plodded, "Ho ho, they say I'm old and slow, but unlike those that to and fro, straight and true is the path I go, with little to no imbroglio . . ."

"You talk as ponderously as you walk," Molly said with flagging patience.

"And thus the voice of reckless haste," it droned. "Why, never to move another inch would be more to my taste.'

"But where would that get us?"

"Cemented, contented, salubrious."

So Molly resigned herself to follow, deciding some progress was better than nothing, although she periodically laid down with eyes closed and napped, then quickly caught up when she woke. And all the while the turtle repeated its mantra, "Ho ho, they say I'm old and slow . . ."

After a day and night they reached a stand of trees that had been a distance of perhaps a few dozen yards from her encounter with the puppy. And now the tortoise stopped and began to draw its head within its shell. "After all this duress, I shall now declare a recess."

"Wait!" Molly shouted. "Have we much farther to go? Point the direction I should take, I'll proceed on my own."

"Why, we have arrived." The tiresome beast sighed. "A brilliant mind awaits us just within this wood. Your questions will be answered, but first, rest would be good."

"You are nothing but a master of delay!" She stomped a foot. "This short distance we've covered, you could have simply told me the way. I'd have had my answers yesterday!"

But the turtle had drawn entirely into its shell.

She strode past into the copse and almost stumbled over a man seated at a table nursing a tankard. He glared and took a swig.

"Oh, pardon me, sir. This may sound strange, but a large, odd tortoise promised to arrange for me to meet here a scholar who could explain the artifacts of Alterland."

He gave her a beady-eyed stare. "Led you here?"

"Why, yes. Promised answers to my questions about alternative facts."

"And by what right," he belched, "would you question me, just to be clear?"

"Well, it's not so much by right as a matter or curiosity, to be exact."

"So, with hypotheticals my words you'll commandeer?"

"Oh, just answer me this. Are you this eminence I'm supposed to contact?"

He hiccupped. "'Tis not something I'm prepared to volunteer."

"Is there no one in this place," Molly said with clenched fist, "who can answer a question direct?"

The man gazed in his tankard and mused a moment. "I like beer."

"How is that relevant?"

"It may be, some day. But I'll answer no more questions, so be on your way."

"But you haven't answered a single question!"

"Oh, and yet I have. Just not one you posed." A bit of foam glistened on his nose.

"Just tell me about Alterland. What harm could there be in such a discussion?"

"My dear, I aspire to lofty position." He flecked away the foam and had another guzzle. "I'll not go on record lest it harm my disposition."

"I might as well banter with Felicity Dillary."

One besotted eyebrow arched. "Who's that you mention?"

"Just a know-it-all in the land above who drives me to dissension."

"And whom, I surmise, you'd like to pillory!" A chuckle was followed by another belch. "Just continue apace, you'll find others quite eager to see her disgraced."

"Others who find her pedantic and boring!" she squealed, but the drunkard had already succumbed to snoring.

3. Strange Words - Egg and Bird

Onward into the wood she trudged, earnestly nursing her grudge. But the woods soon became more a thicket with trees, full of brambles and lichens and thorns and things that crawled and crept. Her shoes grew muddy, her dress disheveled. "I almost wish," Molly grumbled, "I were back in Lubberlay."

"What say?" A spindly man she had not before noticed spun on his heels and thrust a protruding chin in her direction. "That land of moral decay?"

"That seems to me rather an exaggeration."

"And yet," he stated gravely, "these weeds through which you struggle are naught but the product of the tyranny of regulation."

Molly extricated herself from a particularly thorny bush. "I'll have you know, we've none of this underbrush in Lubberlay."

"My point, exactly! Why, even its parkland reeks of freedom's deprivation."

"I fail to see the connection with this underbrush impeding my way."

He bowed his head sadly. "'Tis Lubberlay's restrictive codes prevent men of capital from clearing this wood, extracting from beneath something good."

"Cutting down a forest to get rid of a few weeds seems an overreaction."

"Such ignorance as yours," he said with upturned lip, "requires didaction."

Beckoning her closer, he made a bow-legged turn and sauntered with a professorial air of satisfaction.

"With careful reading doth our constitution construe
Obligations and rights all are bound unto,
Most importantly, the imperative to eschew
The needs of the many for the wants of the few."

"Wait a minute." Molly puzzled a moment. "That sounds like you've got it backwards."

"Economics is not for simpletons, little pickle."

"But don't the needs of the many deserve our regards?"

"Not at all." A smirk. "Reward the rich, the rest receive their trickle."

And with that he faced a nearby wall and undid his trousers.

Miss Malice did blush and covered her browsers.

A voice from above interrupted. "Restrain yourself, blunderball. Besmirch not my beautiful wall!"

Molly looked up and stifled a squeak. Perched atop sat an egg that continued to speak.

"I could not help but overhear your economic ramblings queer. Such thoughts will fall on deafened ears without a brilliant sloganeer."

"Harumph!" The man stroked his prominent chin. "I'll not cheapen my discourse . . ."

"Said the rump of the horse!" The talking egg cackled, then grinned lewdly at Molly. "Are you, lovely lips, taken in by this prattle?"

"I remain a sceptic," she declared. "But neither am I impressed by an egg teetering on a wall . . ."

"Beautiful wall," it interjected.

". . . when so precarious a perch might lead to a fall."

The chinned man smirked. "He deserves his plight."

"Tis true," whined the egg, "I would glad alight."

"Then take my hand," Molly offered. "I will help you down."

"I'd rather someone taller." It frowned.

"You're in no position to be choosy."

It reached past her hand. "Think, instead, I'll grab your . . ."

But a brick slipped and the bad egg stumbled and would have cracked, save onto Molly it tumbled, knocking her down and eliciting yet another "Drumpf!"

Then rolled atop her, head, back, rump.

"Get off me," she cried, "Show a bit of respect!"

It stood, brushed itself off. "Seems I owe you a debt."

Molly scowled. "You do, I daresay."

"By the way, debts are something I never repay."

"Scoundrel!" blurted the skinny-legged man. "That's mere theft!"

"Said the loser," the egg shouted, "with the disgusting cleft."

Finding a stool, the oval creature climbed atop and did continue.

"Your face is foul, your hair stringy, your eyes aren't even blue.

No doubt, your mother lived in a shoe, you rancid, traitorous son of a parvenue!"

On tiptoes it teetered to reach the man's ear, shouting insults therein that were dreadful to hear, a crescendo of profanities, but something rather queer led the mad thing to topple again on its back, yet this time not on Molly, but on a stone, thus, "crack!"

First just a hairline, then more of a fracture spread across its smooth surface.

"This is a disaster!" It cried, just before it split into pieces.

"Well, that's an end to that horrible thesis." Cleft-chin seemed not too displeased.

"Hang on." Molly noticed a stirring. "Why, there's something emerging!" A tiny snout poked out from the shards, sniffing the air in exploration. There followed a head and two hooves.

Cleft-chin laughed. "It would seem the offspring a swine doth prove!"

"But this poor little piglet is all alone, no mother, no home." Molly felt a surge of sympathy, pity for the poor creature thrust by accident into the world. "Oh, sir, we must help this creature find its way."

"'Twould violate the laws of nature. Coddle it now, it will have its hands out forever."

"Hands? What hands?"

"Metaphorical ones, of course." The man raised an eyebrow. "Your emotional liberalism might nourish a stripling but will starve it of initiative and ambition."

"Surely," Molly protested, "You would not abandon an innocent to its doom?"

"Innocence, my dear, dies upon leaving the womb."

"Womb? What womb? It hatched from an egg."

"And a rather distasteful egg at that, I might add." And off the man swaggered; well, as much as a spindly-legged man can.

25

Yet Molly admitted to herself that it was a strange thing, a piglet hatching from an egg, and might call into question many of her assumptions about the nature of things. Still, it seemed a harmless, frightened little creature. She knelt and reached out to pat its head. It scrambled into her lap, then began rubbing up against her in what she deemed an inappropriate manner.

"Why, stop. How disgusting. Just like your father!" Had the egg been male, she wondered? An egg, after all, would seem more a feminine thing. But its crass behavior had definitely been masculine. "This is proving to be a bother! Oh, I can't leave you here all alone, little piggie." She picked it up and nestled it in her arms, then set out to find help.

It grew heavy as she walked. "How can it be," she asked herself, "that this little burden might tire me so? Yet I see it is not weakness; rather, little piggie, you continue to grow." Indeed, the creature was now almost half her size, with dangly legs, a belly, and saucers for eyes. "I hope we find assistance soon, for I doubt I can carry you much longer."

"What's that you've got there, rumor monger?"

Molly noticed a woman with a large head and larger hat seated off to one side. How had she not noticed her before? "What's that you called me?"

"I took you for a journalist, all dressed up and pushy," the woman replied with an air of annoyance. "But the infant you carry, I will take it, verily."

"Infant? Why, it's simply a little pig." But the woman had plucked it from Molly's grasp, and indeed it had transformed into something resembling a baby, a horrid, squalling baby, Molly noted.

"This suckling requires rearing as only I, a princess, may do."

"You are a princess?"

"It's a title. Do you question my qualifications? Yet you carried the golden child like a sack of vegetation."

"Golden child?" Molly scoffed. "To me it seems a bit wan."

"You've never heard of spray tan?" The princess glowered. "Now be gone while I prepare this one for exercise of power."

"Don't you think that a bit premature?"

"I sense a grasping for authority in its nature."

"Well, if it's like its forebear, I doubt it's authority it wants to grasp."

"Whatever." The princess waved her hand in a dismissive gesture. A choking mist filled the air. Molly's eyes teared up. She gasped for breath, stumbled about until she managed to escape the fog.

"Foolish girl!" A man with what seemed to be a cast-iron kettle on his head strode toward her. "Didn't you see the sign?"

"What sign?" she coughed.

"Why, this sign, of course." He turned around to show a piece of posterboard attached to a serving tray hanging on his back. On it was printed, CS GAS TESTING ZONE.

"How would I see the sign if you didn't post it?"

"Oho," said kettle-head. "A conundrum! That's a different bird altogether."

"What do you mean?" Molly asked.

"He means," came a nasally reply, "that such questions are more suited to a deliberative body." And there stood, indeed, a different bird, altogether gangly and odd of appearance. "Yet the question you pose," it continued, "is not so much a conundrum as a hypothetical."

"Tarnation!" exclaimed kettle-head. "Best I take my leave and resume fumigation. Gotta keep these varmints and pests on the run."

"What pests do you counter with tear gas?" Molly queried.

"Why, m'dear, disaffected ones." He lumbered off.

She turned her attention back to the bird. "Will you just stand there while he sprays this field with toxins?"

"Another hypothetical, I fear. I'll not be by silly questions deterred."

"Just what is hypothetical about that large cloud of gas?"

"Why, I'm surprised you even need to ask!" The bird arched its long neck in indignation. "I see only clear sky o'er an empty tract."

"Are you blind or simply lying?"

"I'm afraid you are confused." The bird cast her a pitying glance. "In Alterland, reality is whate'er you choose."

"I get to choose what's real?"

"Well, not you *per se*. When I say you, I mean me. And others who share my complacency."

A tinge of mist carried by wind wafted past. Molly teared up again. The bird sneezed. "It would appear," Molly interjected, "that this pollutant you choose to ignore remains rather irksome."

"Nonsense, my girl. 'Tis but a bit of pollen makes your eyes swollen. But I'll waste no more time on you. I've much too much nothing to do!" And off the bird bounded, leaving Molly alone with her question unanswered.

"Why, everyone I meet here in Alterland is skilled only in the art of deflection!"

4. I Say, I Say, a Gabaway

"Come over here," came a cry, "and tell me that directly, Little Miss Ice Crystal!"

She glanced all around until she espied someone sitting at the far end of the field. "Well, I certainly shall." Walking with a determined stride, she soon made out a small man with a hat as big as his head, seated at a table with an empty cup and plate and an empty-headed looking associate.

"You're late," the imp muttered. "We've been awaiting our tea since half past eight."

"And you'll wait longer," Molly retorted. "I'm not a waitress."

"Then you're of no use at all. The world is made of two kinds, you see, those who are deserving, and those who do the serving. You are clearly not the former and neglect to do the latter."

"That would make three kinds, then, wouldn't it?"

He tossed his head back and considered a moment. "It might, but I choose not to count the rest. As a pundit, I am required to resist complexity. I employ my mental dexterity in the pursuit of simplicity."

"Pundit?" Molly asked. "Is that an official title?"

"It is an elected position." He cocked his hat to the other side. "I am acclaimed so by the voices of the silent majority."

"If they're silent, how do you know they acclaim you as Pundit?"

"Ah, but they have not objected to my assumption of office."

"Well, I am objecting now."

"And by doing so announcing yourself to be in the minority."

"How's that?"

"The silent majority are, well, silent, you see. That is the nature of democracy."

Molly considered the statement a moment. There seemed a certain logic to it. What had she thought so often back in Lubberlay, that those who talked most too frequently got their way, like Felicity Dillary droning on endlessly. Still: "But if they stay silent, how are their voices to be counted to see if they're really a majority?"

The hatted pundit rolled his eyes. "And now you sound like Queen Tewbee."

"Alterland is soon to have a queen?"

"What makes you say that?" He seemed taken aback.

"You just now referred to a queen-to-be."

"Not a queen-to-be, you dolt," he shot back, pointing to a tree by the clearing. "Queen Tewbee. She's standing just over there."

"A tree is named Queen Tewbee?"

"Behind the tree. She's hiding from me." A smug expression contorted his face. "She is the vilest of criminals and fears my insightful questioning will expose her numerous misdemeanors and felonies."

"Oh, dear!" Molly cried. "What has she done?"

He arched an eyebrow. "Tinted her hair with colors that run!"

"That's not exactly a crime, I think."

"Then how's this," he countered with a demonstrative wave. "She pens letters in non-approved ink!"

"You can't be serious. These are hardly infractions."

"And yet she refuses to give satisfaction. Let her provide her correspondence, if she's nothing to hide."

"A valid point," Molly admitted.

"Go and ask her to explain. She's only a few paces away."

"Couldn't you go and ask her yourself?"

He raised his hat in indignation. "I think not. I have my dignity!"

"Ah, well," Molly thought. What harm yet another detour in her Alterland sojourn? She set out toward the tree. After all, she'd never had the chance to question a Queen.

"And should you see a waitress' station," called the pundit, "return with my libation."

"Not likely," she muttered, approaching the tree. A face peered through the branches suspiciously. Molly called out, "You must be Queen Tewbee."

"Must we?" came an answer. "An imperative?"

"Don't be so sensitive." Molly's irritation rose. "I've simply come to ask if you're this Queen who refuses to answer questions."

"What a suggestion!" Out stepped a woman in stately regalia, but her hair was indeed mottled. "Or are you as well obsessed with literary paraphernalia?"

"I'm simply curious why a public figure would object to scrutiny."

"It is no matter for you or him," she pointed to the hatted pundit with disdain, "that we choose a felt-tip with blue ink when we scribble."

It seemed a minor enough matter, Molly had to admit. Yet something about the woman irked her. "Where's the harm if a different ink would make everyone content?"

"And next we suppose you would have it so we must use a ball point. How droll. But we've campaigning to do." She turned her back and stooped a bit. "There's a spot of our hair that we fear is in disrepair, but we cannot see back there. Will you be so kind?"

"What do you have in mind?"

"Why, girl! Have a look and tell us if the dye has took."

Molly squinted. "I see blues and browns and roots of gray."

"Oh, drat and dismay! We must look our best today! Pray, make something of this fray!"

"You're not making much sense," Molly commented.

37

"Arrange the hair so we don't look old. Is that so hard to understand? Do what you're told."

"Well, aren't you the bossy one!" Yet she tugged on a hair here and there. "That'll have to do."

"We thank you, and our constituents, too."

A low, hissing sound erupted behind Molly. Queen Tewbee went quite pale.

"Constituents?" The hissing became a cacophony of evil laughter. "You will have none in jail!"

Molly turned. A creature like nothing she had seen before emerged from the underbrush.

"Don't look it in the eye," whispered the Queen, "for the Gabaway may turn your reason to mush."

"Too late, my pretty," the creature snarled. "The polls are finished. A spigot sits in the bog. Declared victory is at hand excessively. The emperor is modeling a new suit."

"Why, it's speaking nonsense!" Molly exclaimed.

"That's what it does, the Gabaway." Queen Tewbee sat on a stump, suddenly tired. "But, what hey, monster, the election is done? Did I miss it already without having really run?"

"All done!" it shrieked. "A landslide mandate for the great protector."

"I'd have thought," mused the Queen, "the margins closer."

"Of voters, yes," the Gabaway snorted, "but instead were counted Electors."

"How is that democratic?" Molly demanded. "Who picks them?"

From all around came a reply. "In Alterland, little one, they are selected by majorities or minorities, depending on who might be thereby affected."

"Wait," Molly asked, confused. "Which of you said that."

"Why, I did," answered Queen Tewbee and the Gabaway in unison. "'Tis in the constitution, if viewed in the proper perspective. Or otherwise, if not."

"I'd like to read this document," Molly muttered.

"W-wouldn't we all," Queen Tewbee stuttered. "But if I'm smart, I'll depart."

With that, she vanished. The Gabaway cackled. "Discretion, indeed, making way for the new authority. And here it be!"

The haze cleared, revealing a platform full of figures, one prominent and bellowing.

"Behold, my hair!

There's greatness there!

Oh, so much I've done,
more than a
megaton!

I am the
chosen one!

They questioned
my wits:
I created
beautiful deficits!

Where once was compromise, now nought but strife in Alterland; much more in store when leader for life, well spray-tanned!"

"But I know him," cried Molly. "He was just a rotten egg, then an infant swine and a bawling babe!"

"Ah, he is all those things and so much more," crooned the Gabaway. "His reign has led to decades of prosperity and jobs galore!"

"Wait. When was he elected?"

"Several hours ago," the Gabaway intoned.

"Why, then, it's a lie that he's done those things."

The Gabaway shook sadly it's scaly head. "Oh, foolish one, there are no lies in Alterland. Instead . . ."

"Oh, yes," Molly interrupted. "Alternative facts. I get it."

"You certainly will," voices squeaked. Molly whirled. An odd pair stood alarmingly close, glaring.

"Is that supposed to be a threat?"

"It might be so considered," said one.

"Beware, lest we be triggered," said the other.

"We are mighty and mightier than you," said the first, and the second muttered, "We are fierce, the worst."

"I don't doubt that," Molly taunted, "one single bit. I'm certain I've never seen such a pair of twits."

"Hit her," said one.

"You first," said the other.

"You're the eldest."

"You're younger."

"All the more reason why you should start."

"But I'm the one who's smart."

"Prove it."

"You prove it."

As they bickered, Molly noticed the Gabaway had disappeared, as had the podium and its speaker. A breeze with a sour tinge tickled her cheek. Turning, she walked into it, toward what, she did not know.

"She's getting away!" shouted the one.

"After her!" cried the other.

"I'll follow you."

"Not if I do, too."

Molly considered making haste, but reasoned the twits not much of a danger. Unexpectedly, though, she made out a rider on horseback approaching. What sun penetrated the mists and chemical fog glinted off shiny armor. A knight?

"The investigator," shrieked the first twit. "Flee!"

"Not before me," exclaimed the second. And they were gone.

5. [REDACTED]

The knight and horse approached slowly. Ponderously, it seemed to Molly. The horse appeared tired. So, too, the knight, his lined face drooping in a frown as he reined in the aging stallion.

"I wanted a word with them." He sighed.

"Well," stated Molly, "avoiding you was all they could agree on."

"As do so many these days, it would seem." He leaned forward in his saddle, teetered a bit, then righted himself. "And who would you be?"

"Molly Malice of Lubberlay. I chanced upon a finely dressed rabbit and fell down his hole."

"Not pertinent, I'm afraid. I'll be on my way." He moved to spur his horse, swaying precipitously before righting himself again. The horse snorted, lowered its snout and commenced loudly grazing. "Ah, I fear my mount does not embrace this inquiry."

"That's right. One of the twits said you're an investigator."

The knight pulled himself erect. "Inquisitor Plenipotentiary, to be precise."

"Then into what, exactly, are you inquiring?"

"Malfeasance. Collusion. Corruption. Impropriety."

"Well, from what I've seen," Molly commented, "Alterland could use a serious house-cleaning."

The knight looked concerned. "Why, that is not my mandate. I am charged to investigate and make recommendations only."

"Recommendations? To whom?"

"I cannot say until my report has been written, transcribed, and redacted."

"Redacted?"

"Sensitive information removed."

"Is much of the information you've gathered sensitive?"

"Almost all of it."

"Well, have you at least found evidence of wrongdoing?"

"No need," the Knight said solemnly. "Malfeasance and collusion with a malevolent actor are widely acknowledged."

"Oh, then you're planning to level charges?"

The question elicited a raised eyebrow and another teeter. "That is not in my mandate. And the actor is foreign, and therefore beyond my jurisdiction."

"Too bad you can't reach him, then."

"Indeed." The knight nodded, then pointed. "And said actor is just there now."

Molly whirled to see. There stood a frightful creature in conversation with . . . "I know that turtle!"

"Yes, one of Alterland's prominent officials."

"Why, they're colluding as we speak! Why don't you stop them?"

"As I mentioned," answered the knight gravely, "I will write my report with all detailed and hand it to the relevant authorities . . ."

"I suggest you do so quickly."

". . . just as soon as it has been fully redacted."

"Made useless, you mean. I've lost patience with you." Molly spun from the knight and strode toward the tortoise and monster, determination in her eye. "Hey, terrapin, you seem to have emerged from your shell!"

The turtle made no reply. As Molly neared, she noted this new creature seemed more fierce than even the dreaded Gabaway, talons menacing. It beat its wings and puffed out its chest. "Do not meddle in what you know not, *malyshka*."

"My name is Molly Malice, not Malyshka!"

"Mollishka, then. Begone, meddlesome one. Your betters have business to conduct." It waggled a talon in her direction.

"Not until I learn what you're plotting with this tortoise." Molly turned defiantly to the creature. "And just what are you supposed to be and what is your purpose?"

"Why, I am the Pyuton, Ruler of Polonia. And I have no porpoise, though in my country are many sturgeon."

"Purpose, not porpoise."

"Turtle, not tortoise," the bespectacled terrapin interjected. "Haven't I seen you somewhere before?"

"You don't remember me?" Molly laughed. "It's been merely hours since we last spoke!"

The Pyuton hissed. "Memories are short in Alterland, fortunately. Before this term, 'twere many a pachyderm with better recall made us squirm. But they met their fate. The new species are more prone to cooperate."

"Cooperate in what?" Molly asked.

"Why, ensuring that Alterland deteriorates, of course. To the benefit of Polonia."

Surprised by the monster's candor, Molly turned to the turtle. "Surely you heard that! This creature is an enemy of your state!"

"Why, yes," it drawled, "make Alterland great."

"You old fool!"

"A quite useful tool," the Pyuton crooned. "And others, too, willingly serve as our vestibule."

Shocked, Molly muttered, "How have you found so many amenable to treason?"

"Money. *Kompromat*. There's many a reason." It chuckled. "But mostly they were grateful for what I teach them."

"Oh, what's that?"

"Being outvoted in elections need not lead to ejections."

His words made sense in a hypnotic way, confusing Molly. "But then, what's the point of elections?"

"Old Polonian saying: identify your opposition, then polonium them." The Pyuton smiled a wicked smile.

"Polonium's a verb?"

"And much, much more." The creature produced a small thermos. "Would you like some tea?"

"No, thank you." Molly turned and left, hastily, thinking to herself that things seemed greatly amiss in Alterland. She longed for the quieter times of Lubberlay. Even Felicity Dillary was beginning to seem less infuriating. She checked her hair; relief, her comb was still there.

6. A Monarch (not a butterfly)

A hubbub of voices intruded on her reflections. Curious, she moved toward the noise, slowly making out figures seated around a table. It seemed to be a hearing of sorts. A familiar voice bellowed.

"Remove these peaches at once, scalawags!"

A waiflike figure responded: "The peach meant something in loftier times. Each peach will teach the lessons of freedom from despotism!"

"How dare you impugn my beauty, leeches!"

"Peaches!" shouted the triumvirate of accusers.

"I have god-like powers! Divine! Prometheus!"

"Tyrant! We have brought the peaches!"

One man sat silently at the table, reading and seemingly paying little attention. Molly sidled up to him.

"Please, sir, can you explain this hullabaloo?"

He looked up. "Why, it is the traditional impeachment."

"Traditional?" Molly wondered if maybe she had misheard. "I had always thought impeachment rare."

"Perhaps in times long past. But it has become ceremonial since the days of King Tewbee." He returned to his book.

"King Tewbee? I've met a queen by that name."

He sighed, looked up. "Yes, it would seem the ladies no longer content to clean and cook."

Molly arched an eyebrow indignantly. "And that is sexist, all the same!"

"Semantics," muttered the man. "Now leave me in peace. 'Tis hard enough reading with all this racket."

"Well, if it's quiet you seek, why not leave for a field or thicket removed from this procedure."

"I cannot."

"Oh, why is that?"

He shook his head slowly, sadly. "I am, by order, the presiding officer."

"Shouldn't you be paying attention, then?"

"No need," he noted with exasperation, "until witness testimony begins."

"That makes sense." Mollified, Molly relaxed. "And when is that expected to start?"

"Never. The jurors decided hearing evidence would not be smart."

Molly was taken aback. "What kind of trial allows jurors to decide whether or not they will hear testimony or review evidence?"

The man gave her a quizzical glance. "You are aware that you stand on the sovereign soil of Alterland, perchance?"

"I'd almost forgotten. That explains a lot."

"Now quiet, child," the man said with a dismissive gesture. "Members of the jury are about to speak. First up, the Duchess of Doublespeak."

A woman of serious demeanor and garments in need of a dry-cleaner arose and with a haughty air declaimed:

"So much has been discerned. Of abuse and treachery we have learned. This despot hath truth and decorum spurned. His wickedness, his criminality is confirmed. I have no recourse but to acquit. I am gravely concerned."

"Wait." Confused, Molly could not restrain herself. "You've described a reign of terror! Surely your vote of not guilty is in error!"

"Whatever are you talking about, young lady?" the Duchess asked dismissively. "The tyrant has learned his lesson. Freed of restraints, he will now ease his oppression."

A familiar voice wafting on a breeze whispered in Molly's ear. "Perhaps now you understand alternative facts."

"Why, Felicity Dillary, I think I do. Up is down. White is black!"

"Racism!" came a cry from the gallery. "I trumpet your perfidy!"

Indeed, an odd half-hare of a man, oddly dressed with odd face and hair, holding a trumpet, oddly, stood and commenced to nattering.

"Of liberty I speak this day, liberty that shall be taken 'way if authority were left to fray in anarchy. Pray preserve my liberty to bray incessantly against the sway of objectionists that seek to stay our leader's apparent moral decay."

"That's the most nonsensical speech I've heard as yet," Molly commented.

"Admirable, indeed!" The terrapin appeared as if from thin air. "His words express better than any I have uttered the benefits of all action shuttered."

"But surely you cannot believe obstruction and inaction appropriate in all matters?"

"The public prism doth but impede the budding red rose of capitalism. See now how the natural order adorns the landscape, loosed by the defeat of regulatory liberalism." The reptile smugly waved a paw toward a rose garden attended by three blustering pages.

Molly squinted in disbelief. "Those are not red roses."

"You lie!" shouted the gardeners. "They are a beautiful red for all to espy."

"Are you color-blind?" Molly pointed. "They're white."

"They turn glorious red as day becomes night!" And, indeed, a few roses became crimson.

"Why, you're painting them. To what end?"

All three returned menacing glowers. "Red roses were promised, friend."

"That paint will suffocate them.'

"They'll have served their purpose by then."

"And what purpose might that be?"

They bowed their heads and intoned, "Adorn the installation of a new emperor for the nation."

The smallest of the three began to jump and shout. "There comes now the attendant with the crown!"

"So it comes to this," Molly shrieked with horror. "You abandon your republic for a noxious tyranny!"

"Readily! Eagerly! Joyously!" exulted the three.

A murmur went up, a few voices of discontent expressing dissent, only to be drowned out by the now ascendant, spray-tanned King Malevolence.

"Call out my militias to keep this rabble in line. Allow no protests while I claim what is mine!"

A thin-lipped courtesan emerged from the crowd. King Malevolence paused, bowed. "The titles are yours," stated the Lady. "By right and Pre-nup claim I the rest."

The King rose up. "I protest!"

"Neither by storm nor incest will I concede. Be best"

An uneasy quiet ensued, and Molly saw a chance to intrude.

"How unseemly, this squabble over jewels and titles, unmerited baubles belonging by right to the common revenue."

"Ho!" smirked the Lady. "I really don't care. Do you?"

"Not so fast!" A girl pushed through the crowd and snatched the crown. "This gets passed to me. You promised, Daddy!"

"Not yet, my pet." The would-be King flushed, Molly could see, through gaps in his orange blush.

"I've paid in trade for that bauble, bitch!" shrieked the courtesan.

"What makes you think I haven't, witch?" retorted the maiden.

The Duchess waved her hands in dismay. "I must avert my eyes and maintain ignorance of this unpleasant display. I cannot in good conscience witness such corruption and not turn away; must hope all subsides one day."

A crier's voice interrupted the fray. "All quiet now for the commencement of the Fawning!"

Silence fell as members of the entourage assumed positions of obeisance around the King. Cries erupted all around.

"Your magnificence knows no bounds!"

"We are in awe of your genius!"

"What power! What manliness!"

"Before you life was meaningless!"

"Wow! You're terrific!"

"How disgusting," Molly said under her breath. "I think I'm feeling sick."

"Shut your yap!" shouted one of the twits. She had missed their arrival. Indeed, all Alterland seemed present. "Comments such as yours will be suppressed."

"But I am feeling distressed," Molly pleaded. "There's something strange in the air, a whiff of despair."

"I fear it's more than that," interjected a small man bearing a missive making his way through the crowd. "Make way! Make way! I've important news for the King!"

The crowd quieted. The King turned toward the interloper. "What, have you brought accolades from other despots? Do they acknowledge I am now the envy of all the world?"

"Not exactly." The man extended the brocaded envelope matter-of-factly. "'Tis more an event I thought you should be aware of."

"A festival to honor me? An invitation to address the world stage, reveal my genius and wisdom sage?"

"Well, since you won't read the notice, I'll speak plainly." The man appeared mildly irritated. "Pandemic."

The King seemed confused. "Is this some new word of praise? I prefer more traditional ones."

"Pandemic!" The man commenced to shout. "Disease! Virus! Plague!"

"Nonsense!" retorted the King. "All in Alterland is naught but greatness, thanks to my munificence and brilliance."

"PANDEMIC!" shouted the man. "PLAGUE!"

"Hush." The King's eyes darted back and forth. "Everyone will hear you. And by what right do you spread such alarm?"

"I am director of the Institute for Disease and Bodily Harm."

"Hang on. If I remember, my first act as Autocratist was to fire all the scientists!" The King summoned security. "Remove this alarmist!"

"Be aware," shouted the man as they dragged him away, "your alternative facts cannot stay disease. It does not care."

A worried murmur passed through the crowd made uneasy by the sudden appearance of reality.

"Fear not, verily," soothed the monarch. "Like magic, and said scientists, this will disappear. My most trusted adviser so assures me. Bring him here!"

A pale individual in ridiculous costume emerged from the crowd. Until that moment, Molly had assumed him a jester.

"Oh, simple folk," he announced, "there is much less danger than it might look. Our great King has banished illness. No doubt this fool mistook a minor flu for something serious. I am no scientist, of course, but I have read several books."

"Nevertheless, shouldn't we take precautions, just in case?" came a shout. A scuffle ensued, the malcontent removed from the place.

"The invisible hand of the market will vanquish any threat," the adviser continued. "Action by the crown can do little to abet private industry, though, yet, it is advisable for men of capital to seek profit in this atmosphere of uncertainty. A good bet is to stockpile medicines, then withhold them, since our enemies may be most beset."

"Why, he's almost as smart as me," the King crooned. "You see, there is no need to worry, folks. I hereby declare this Pandemic a Hoax!"

A cheer erupted from the multitude; dancing ensued. Molly, however, was not mollified, especially as many cheers transformed into paroxysms of coughing. *I think I'd best be away from here*, she realized. Others felt the same, it seemed, slipping quietly into the nearby wood. Yet from somewhere came a horrible beast blocking their egress.

"Desist!" it growled. "No recess from glorifying the leader is permitted. Return to the fawning or for stocks be fitted!"

7. Behemoth

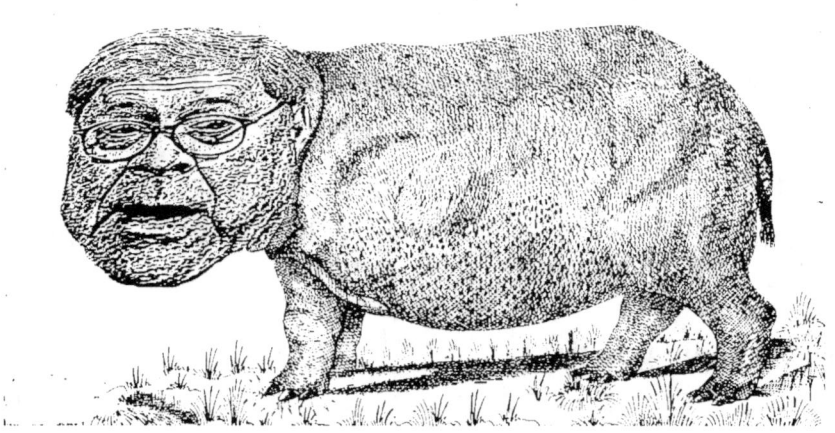

The beast pawed the earth and snorted a noxious cloud. Panicked, the throng turned 'round, made its way back to alternative ground. Yet many collapsed, fever now spreading as a wildfire by leaps and bounds. Cries of "plague!" and "pandemic!" echoed from the suffering mass.

"Take care such words be muted," brayed the beast, "lest you be prosecuted."

"Can't you see they're falling ill?" Molly demanded. "Stop bullying them, you disgusting animal."

"Anarchist!" shouted the beast, charging. Molly turned and ran as fast as she could. But the sound of stomping hooves behind her stopped abruptly. She looked back. The beast had halted, out of breath.

"You . . . cannot escape . . . enemy of the state!" It gasped.

"Perhaps not, if you weren't so fat!" She laughed. "Or maybe this plague has caught up to you."

"You won't . . . feel so . . . elated . . . once you are . . . incarcerated." It sat and panted some more.

"You're welcome to try, Lardbard."

"Socialist!"

Molly skipped through the forest, pleasant at last with no monsters or blathering creatures obscuring its more tolerable features. "You know," she mused, "if it weren't for the occupants, Alterland would not be so bad."

She tripped over a log, tumbled down a hill, and fell into a mound of coarse sand.

"Who dares trespass here?" a voice said.

Molly looked up. "It's a beach. Why would entry be prohibited?"

"This is the shore by the Shining Sea, not to be confused with the seashore," stated a tusked man of significant girth. "Intruders to Alterland are detained, lest our purity be stained."

"If this is not the seashore, then what's that sea over there?"

"Fool," cried the Tusked Man's associate. "This is the Shining Sea. The seashore is by the Sea on the other side of Alterland, which stretches from Sea to Shining Sea."

"That's a song lyric, not an internationally binding definition of territorial rights," Molly pointed out.

"And yet, I'll wager, you're no more well versed in legalese than these illegal border crossers we have corralled," replied the shriveled, hatted of the two.

"Why, these are nothing but shellfish," Molly objected.

"Mollusks," stated Tusk Man imperiously. "Bivalve mollusks of the semi-sentient variety."

"How long do you plan to keep them imprisoned here?"

"Why, they will be deported anon," muttered the one with drooping facial features, distractedly.

"Back to the sea?"

"We shall see."

"Please set us free!" shouted the oysters. Molly was taken aback by the pitiful racket.

"I would like to speak," Molly stated, "to someone in authority."

"Be careful what you wish for," said Tusk Man. "But in yonder hut is an expert on legalities, if you wish to complain."

"I most certainly do. And much more I'd like to have explained." Molly made her way with renewed determination. "Maybe I'll finally get to the bottom of this Alterland abomination."

A crone with a glint in her eye emerged from the hut. "Well, who is this skinny creature come calling abrupt?"

"I'm Molly Malice, and I've been inquiring about alternative facts."

"Lard is better."

"What?"

"Than alternative fats." The crone grinned slyly. "Or bacon drippings. Mmmm."

"Facts!"

"What good are those?"

"To distinguish," Molly offered, "between what is and is not real."

"Better a tasty porridge to fatten you up, make of you a juicier meal."

Molly recoiled in shock. "You were recommended for advice legal, not as some kind of cannibal."

"Semantics." The crone waved her stick. "But I haven't been a lawyer in ages. Found other work, pays better wages."

"Still, are you aware of the gulag being run on this very beach?"

"Well, that's a bit of a reach. I've seen those facilities," came her retort. "Not so much detention camp as holiday resort."

"The inmates disagree."

"They're oysters, dearie. Not so much inmates as delicacy."

"But they're intelligent!" Molly cried. "I've heard them speak"

"So?" A bit of saliva dribbled across the crone's cheek.

Suddenly in horrified realization, Molly retraced her steps to her earlier location. Too late, she arrived to find devastation. Empty shells lay hither and yon. Tusk Man belched; the droop-faced man yawned.

Molly gasped. "You've eaten them!"

"Whom?"

"The oysters!"

"I see no oysters here," Tusk Man replied. The sagging-skin man added, "Nor do I."

"Then what of all these empty shells?" She pointed all around.

"Abandoned baggage of the dearly deported, perhaps?"

"Or is that departed?" Waggling a tusk, the rotund one sniffed an empty shell.

"An insignificant distinction," Droop-face commented, wiping a barnacle with a piece of bread and taking a bite. "Either way, I'm not quite satisfied."

"There's still hot water in the kettle. Perhaps this irksome girl with a flavoring of nettles?"

"Mmmm."

Molly swore she heard three voices expressing delight, the crone no doubt having followed for a bite. She took her leave politely and retreated apace into the forest whence she came. "Alterland just gets odder and odder. Alternative facts do not, it seems, make intelligent fodder."

8. This Way the Truth Lies

The forest seemed darker, more foreboding than before. She reflected on her journey as she walked. Each new encounter had made accepting absurdity a habit; it no longer seemed strange her adventure began by following a rabbit, stretching beyond the bounds of reason to strange creatures and monsters contemplating treason. Molly shivered to think what might lie ahead, then stumbled onto a path.

"But which way?" she wondered. "Will one direction take me back to Lubberlay?"

"Please hold questions until called on."

"Oh, no. Not another mysterious voice," Molly lamented. "No doubt this will be some siren sent to confuse my choice."

"How rude!" The voice was nasal, feminine. Molly made out an apparition, diffuse at first, then resolving into a disembodied head. "Take care. I only answer questions when I'm in the mood."

"You have serpents instead of hair. Why would I trust your answers?" Molly asked.

"I never lie," stated the apparition. "And those are not serpents. My locks are silky and fair."

The serpents hissed in emphasis. Molly kept her distance. "Your second assertion would seem to call into question your first. But you may be the strangest thing I've encountered yet. What kind of ghost are you, anyway?"

"Whatever of Alterland you seek to know or find, your answer I may provide from my many binders." As she spoke, notebooks with color-coded tabs manifested, floating in the air around her. "To anticipate your first inquiry, let me assure you, no oysters have been harmed or eaten."

"And yet I've seen the evidence with my own eyes!"

"Do not believe the fake media at any time." Forked tongues darted from the snakes' mouths. "They have been complicit covering up Queen Tewbee's crimes."

"This again?" Molly shook her head in disbelief. "You'd think more concern would be shown for the Pyuton's conspiring or how this new plague has grown."

"Hoaxes, both! All Alterland is healthy and content as never before!"

"Oh, my. This lie bodes particularly ill. But tell me, shill, does this path lead to Lubberlay, and if so, which way?"

"Why, no such place exists," she shrieked, "and if it did, this path that twists to your left would take you farther away."

"That's all I needed to know." Molly turned left and set off down the lane.

"Stop!" screamed the apparition. "You must not go that way!"

"Just keep confirming my decision, airhead," Molly muttered.

The path did twist a bit at first, then straightened for a long stretch through woods ever denser and darker. She began to wonder if the snake-headed creature had actually tricked her into taking this direction. But the lies had been so consistent, it had seemed wisest to follow the opposite course advised.

As she walked, she heard a whimpering ahead, first plaintive, then increasingly forlorn. It was a simpering whine, like some child aggrieved at the loss of a favorite toy. She rounded a slight bend and saw the source of the racket. "You, again!"

"Unfair!" The now disheveled King wailed. "Jealousy, that's what it is! Traitors, all!"

"What is it you're carrying on about? You bawl like an infant." Molly could barely contain her disgust.

"They blame me for everything, the death, the economic ruin."

"What did you expect? You sought this monarchy. Didn't you know rulers are held responsible by the ruled?"

"I never accepted to be responsible for anything," he mewled. "I was chosen to be acclaimed for my successes, for my genius."

"To be acclaimed for successes, you actually have to, well, have successes. Did you not realize that?"

"I have announced many victories." He glowered at her.

"Simply proclaiming something doesn't make it true."

He looked confused. "Not in Alterland. Here, facts are whatever you choose."

"It would seem," Molly said, only really grasping it herself at that moment, "reality is the final arbiter, even in Alterland. Ignore it, you lose."

"Fake news," he growled. "I sent my militias to root out the heretics who spread such lies. Bad luck, they all got sick and died."

Molly started to remonstrate, but the ailing figurehead erupted in a fit of coughing. "You've caught this plague as well." Frightened, she backed away.

"'Tis but a mild flu. Come close, I'll show you."

"I think not." She turned and ran. Her heart raced. The forest closed in around her, obscuring the path. She labored to breathe, the atmosphere suddenly thick and fetid. "Oh, has it come to this, I am to fall sick, succumb to a pandemic?"

Her knees buckled and she collapsed with another "Drumpf!" into a darkness that was deep and, well, dark. She felt her consciousness dissipate, strange beasts and contagions swirling all around as the light faded . . .

9. 'Twas All a Dream?

And awoke in her bed, shaking, exhausted, but not in the least dead! Collecting her faculties, she sat up. "What a nightmare that was!" she said.

She stood, shakily at first, then had to step around a beast curled up at the foot of her bed. "And when did I acquire a pet?" she wondered, then noticed in dismay 'twas no canine stray. "Must be a trick of the light, a remnant of my visions in the night to give one last fright."

The Pyuton stretched, yawned, continued sleeping. Molly crept past lightly to keep the floorboards from creaking.

She made her way into the foyer, then on to the study. A welcome sight, Felicity Dillary sat wrapped in a blanket, looking particularly cuddly. Her old nemesis looked up, smiled wanly. "You're finally up."

"How long have I been sleeping?"

"Several days, dear," Felicity said with a sigh of relief. "You had us all worried. 'Tis a virus that's more than a few buried."

"A sickness? That's real? I had thought it a product of my imagination, a vision in the night accompanied by fantastic behemoths, foolish sprites and other creatures skilled only at prevarication." Molly shivered. "I'm glad none of that was real, glad to be safe at home."

A sadness crept o'er Felicity's features. "So you've forgotten."

"What say?"

"The Republic of Lubberlay. It's gone away. Where once shone the sun is now cloudy and gray."

"How?"

"It would seem some deplorables chose to listen to fables." The old woman pointed to the window. "You may have thought you were only dreaming. These days, all of us, we wake up screaming."

Molly looked through the glass and gasped. "Alas, our home is now a graveyard."

"Well, we tried being decent, my pet. But, as things turned out, it was just too hard."

Molly grew sad, then touched her hair, brightened,
reassured.
"Well, at least my Oma's comb is still secured!"

We Wake Up Screaming

About the Author

Not much is known about David E. Manuel. He apparently lives in obscurity, isolating of his own choosing well before the arrival of COVID-19 in America made social distancing a popular fad. Rumor has it that he has been inventing stories for most of his life. Making a career of his penchant for dishonesty, he labored in the shadows for the Central Intelligence Agency some twenty-eight years; at least, he has claimed that on occasion. Given his talent for fabrication, though—evidenced by several novels he allegedly wrote and published—a discerning reader would be cautioned to take such claims with a grain of salt. Of course, a discerning reader doubtless would have abandoned this questionable volume long before reaching this "About the Author" section. Anyway, *caveat lector* and all that. Or, as David has been known to say, "believe whatever you like, as long as you buy the book." He's also been heard muttering, "those are just a few of the birds, Mr. Antrobus," but that's a different matter entirely.

Also by David E. Manuel

The Richard Paladin Series

Killer Protocols

Richard Paladin, licensed to kill. But is his license really valid? And what does any of this have to do with the Kyoto Protocol? Find out by reading this first installment of the Richard Paladin Series.

Clean Coal Killers

Is there really such a thing as clean coal? You won't find out here, but you will meet a few spies, goons, and thugs as well as a gorgeous stripper and a sexy secret agent. What they're doing at a Pennsylvania power plant is...well, you'll have to read the book.

The Killer Trees

Join Richard Paladin in this third, genre-bending installment as he tracks a killer in an Oregon forest.

Something completely different:

Alligator in My Basement

There's an alligator living in Danny Foster's basement, but that's not what has him worried. He's worried one day his wife will realize she's married to a jerk and leave him. He's worried the principal at the middle school where he teaches English will find out he doesn't know what he's doing and fire him. Mostly he's worried that his father was right, that he's a loser who will never amount to anything. The alligator's about the only thing that doesn't have him worried. He's been taking care of it since his father got it years before. But when it escapes its enclosure and takes to sitting at the foot of the basement stairs trying to figure out how to climb them, Danny realizes he's going to have to deal with the single problem he thought he had a handle on. Because an alligator on the loose is the one thing that can shatter Danny's tenuous existence.

Also available from Persimmon Alley Press

Works by Richard L. Hermann

Close Encounters with the Cold War: Personal Battles with Evil Empires, Cold Warriors, and Others

Author Richard Hermann had a front-row seat during the Cold War. Close Encounters with the Cold War: Personal Battles with Evil Empires, Cold Warriors and Others is his bio-history of his and his Cold Warrior colleagues' experiences during that nail-biting half-century.

Mother's Century: A Survivor, Her People and Her Times

is the "bio-history" of Margarete Sobel Hermann, the author's mother and role model, who lived 101 tumultuous and productive years. Her life spanned 95 percent of the twentieth century, during which she and her family experienced much of the good, the bad and the exceptionally ugly that marked that most violent of eras. Born into a middle-class Jewish family in Imperial Vienna, she survived the First World War, famine and starvation, runaway inflation, political turmoil that makes what we are undergoing today pale in comparison, discrimination, street violence, the Great Depression, the Nazi takeover of Austria, the Holocaust during which scores of her relatives perished in the death camps, and the daunting task of getting herself and her family out of Europe to America.

Encounters: Ten Appointments with History

describes ten meetings between historically relevant individuals and, in one case civilizations, that have profoundly imprinted themselves on both their contemporary eras and what followed.

Find these and other books at:
www.persimmonalleypress.com